Sloth Sleeps Over

BLYTHE RUSSO

VIKING

Sloth
5b

Sloth is invited to her very first sleepover!

Now, Sloth hasn't a clue what a sleepover is . . .

but it must involve sleeping, right?

And sleeping is

Sloth's favorite.

She is a superb snoozer. A top-notch napper.

A dutiful dozer.

There is nothing Sloth is better at than sleeping.

And there is nothing Paloma is better at than . . .

. . . not sleeping?

Sloth, this is going to be the best sleepover ever! I can't wait to stay up all night long!

Sloth can barely stay awake through an entire meal, let alone ALL. NIGHT. LONG. Will falling asleep ruin the sleepover?

What a di-ZZZZ-aster!

Nonetheless, it's time for the sleepover to begin.

First up, pizza and ice cream.

Perfect, Sloth thinks.

Pizza is the one meal

she can stay awake for.

Once their bellies are happy, it's time to have some fun!

Paloma introduces Sloth to all of the best games . . .

. . . and Sloth quickly becomes a sleepover professional.

And the best part is she isn't even feeling sleepy.

Not one little bit.

HEAP of SHE

Well, maybe a TEENSY bit sleepy. She just needs a little energy boost. What she needs is a . . .

spontaneous dance party!

After busting all the moves,

it's movie time!

But halfway through the movie . . .

I'M AWAKE!
Can you please pass the popcorn?

Sloth just can't hide it anymore.

She is positively pooped.

Totally tuckered. Solidly spent.

Maybe she can take a catnap! A real quick one.

Paloma won't notice, right?

No, she has to tell Paloma the truth.

Sloths just aren't meant to stay up all night . . .

. . . but maybe neither are Palomas.

Sloth quietly celebrates.

Finally, she thinks,

it's her time to shine.

Best. Sleepover. Ever.
OOPS!

And sleepovers are Sloth's favorite.

For Mom and Dad, every book is for you.
And for Molly, who would have thought?!
(You did and for that I am forever grateful.)

VIKING
An imprint of Penguin Random House LLC, New York

First published in the United States of America by Viking,
an imprint of Penguin Random House LLC, 2022

Visit us online at penguinrandomhouse.com.

Library of Congress Cataloging-in-Publication Data

Names: Russo, Blythe, author, illustrator.
Title: Sloth sleeps over / Blythe Russo.
Description: New York : Viking, 2022 | Audience: Ages 3–5 years. | Audience: Grades K–1.
Summary: Sloth is having her first sleepover at her best friend Paloma's house, but when she finds out at that Paloma plans to stay up all night, sleep-loving Sloth realizes she must find a way to stay awake.
Identifiers: LCCN 2021032143 (print) | LCCN 2021032144 (ebook) | ISBN 9780593350959 (hardcover)
ISBN 9780593350966 (ebook) | Subjects: CYAC: Sloths--Fiction. | Sleepovers--Fiction.
Classification: LCC PZ7.1.R8728 Sl 2022 (print) | LCC PZ7.1.R8728 (ebook) | DDC [E]-dc23
LC record available at https://lccn.loc.gov/2021032143
LC ebook record available at https://lccn.loc.gov/2021032144

Manufactured in China

ISBN 9780593350959

1 3 5 7 9 10 8 6 4 2

HH

Design by Lucia Baez • Text set in Mohr Rounded Alt

The art for this picture book was made using a combination of traditional watercolor paintings scanned and then layered beneath digital linework and other details added in Photoshop.